On the
Spot

BAINTE DEN STOC

WITHDRAWN FROM
DÚN LAOGHAIRE-RATHDOWN COUNTY
LIBRARY STOCK

STADIUM SCHOOL

WHERE FOOTBALLING DREAMS COME TRUE

On the
Spot

Jefferies & Goffe

A & C Black • London

First published 2008 by
A & C Black Publishers Ltd
36 Soho Square, London, W1D 3QY

www.acblack.com

Text copyright © 2008 C. Jefferies and S. Goffe

The rights of C. Jefferies and S. Goffe to be identified as
the authors of this work have been asserted by them in accordance
with the Copyrights, Designs and Patents Act 1988.

ISBN 978-1-4081-0084-4

A CIP catalogue for this book is available from the British Library.

All rights reserved. No part of this publication may be
reproduced in any form or by any means – graphic, electronic
or mechanical, including photocopying, recording, taping or
information storage and retrieval systems – without the
prior permission in writing of the publishers.

This book is produced using paper that is made from wood
grown in managed, sustainable forests. It is natural, renewable
and recyclable. The logging and manufacturing processes conform
to the environmental regulations of the country of origin.

Printed and bound in Great Britain
by CPI Cox & Wyman, Reading, RG1 8EX

Contents

Map of Stadium School

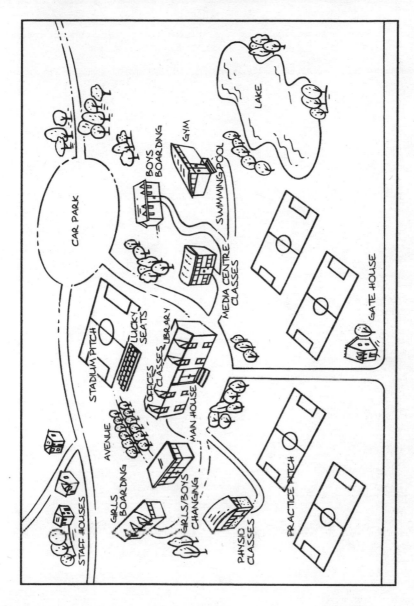

1. Keeper Crisis

Tom Larsson was playing an absolute blinder in goal. He'd made several majestic saves, and it was beginning to seem like he was unbeatable.

It was a chilly winter's morning, and the students were halfway through their training session at top football academy, Stadium School. Mr Jenkins, the junior coach, had split them up to play some practice matches.

"I hope you're not all too full of Christmas pudding," he'd joked at the start of the session. "We've got an 11-week term ahead of us, including a match against Leeds Academy in week six, so you'll need to be in peak condition. But today we're going to

On the Spot

ease you back into the swing of things with a game. Do you all remember the squad I picked at the end of last term?"

Of course everyone could remember. Either from the excitement of getting in, or the disappointment of missing out.

"The first-team defence will play against the first-team attack," Mr Jenkins had explained. "With the rest of the squad filling in the other positions. That way the teams will be fair, and the main units of the first team can practise playing alongside each other. First-team defence will be in bibs, attack in shirts. If that doesn't include you, make your way over to Mrs Powell, who'll be supervising the other match."

It was a great idea, but Roddy Jones and the rest of the shirts were having a very frustrating morning as they tried to break down the bibs' defence. As always when he played a game of football, Roddy's internal commentary was keeping track of the unfolding events.

And it's yet another top-drawer save from Larsson! He's really keeping the bibs in the game today. He throws the ball out to a full-back, but almost immediately possession goes to the shirts and Larsson's goal is under threat again.

Jones moves the ball out to Keira Sanders, who takes it round her marker then knocks it to Bullard on the edge of the box. It's a rasping shot from Bullard, but Larsson somehow gets his fingertips to it and pushes it onto the post. Geno Perotti is lurking for the rebound, and pokes the ball coolly past the keeper, who has no chance to recover. Jimmy Piper, in the bibs' defence, throws himself at the ball, but his last-ditch defending is too late. The ball trickles over the line.

On the Spot

"Yeah! We did it! Goal!" Geno stabbed the air in triumph, but Roddy grabbed his sleeve.

"Tom Larsson's down!" he said. "It looks like he's injured."

Geno turned back towards the goal. Tom Larsson was hunched over, cradling his right hand; he appeared to be in agony. Mr Jenkins was already on the scene and all the players were gathering round.

"Is he all right?" said Geno, anxiously.

"What happened?" asked Keira.

"It must have been that last save," said Jimmy. "His fingers bent right back when he got his hand to it."

Keira winced.

"Sounds bad," said Roddy. "Tom doesn't normally make a fuss when he's hurt."

Mr Jenkins waved them all back, and had a few words with Tom. Then he helped the white-faced goalie slowly to his feet. He radioed to the physio room and it wasn't long before Mrs Anstruther, the school nurse, arrived. She took off Tom's goalie glove carefully and had a quick look at his fingers, but it was obvious that his part in the game was over. Mrs Anstruther spoke briefly to Mr Jenkins, before leading Tom off the pitch.

As soon as Tom and the nurse had left, Mr Jenkins spoke to the rest of the players. "It's likely Tom has a broken finger," he said, "and he won't be match fit for a while. Ashanti, can you run over to the other game and tell Mrs Powell we need Marcel Temperley, please. Unfortunately, injuries do happen sometimes. Now, let's get this game going again."

Everyone went back to their positions for the restart, and waited as Marcel walked slowly across from the other pitch. The

On the Spot

Charlton keeper was third choice behind Tom Larsson and Dij Anichebe, who was playing in goal for the shirts, but the Frenchman didn't seem very keen to grab this chance of making an impression.

"Cheer up, Marcel," Roddy muttered.

"He got very moody last term, and things obviously haven't improved over Christmas," said Geno, as he lined up beside his friend for the kickoff. "I don't think he's very happy here."

Roddy shook his head. "I can't believe *anyone* would be unhappy at Stadium School," he said. "It's football heaven! We were all so lucky to get in. And now we've got a chance to go to the top, with the best coaching and…"

"OK, I know *you* love it," laughed Geno. "And I do, too. But poor Marcel is struggling. Didn't you realise? He can't stand grumpy

Mr Roberts, the goalkeeping coach, *and* he has to share a room with Jack Carr. How would you feel if your roommate was the school bully, and your coach couldn't take a joke?"

Roddy thought about it as the game got underway. If he didn't get on well with his coach, it *would* be a bit of a damper on the fun. And Roddy could see that Jack would be even more of a problem. He was a talented footballer, but he liked to throw his weight around, on *and* off the pitch. Roddy had assumed that Marcel got on OK with Jack, but maybe he didn't. After all, they hadn't *chosen* to share a room.

But whatever was up with Marcel, Roddy had to stop thinking about it on the football pitch, even if it *was* just a practice session. He pushed a pass out to Ashanti on the wing, and started to focus fully on the game.

On the Spot

If Marcel wasn't playing to his best, it would make it much easier for Roddy to score.

Temperley is on in place of the injured Larsson, and he is immediately under pressure. Bullard, Perotti and Marek Dvorski are wreaking havoc in the box, and Temperley is throwing himself around to keep the ball out. A cross comes in from the left, and Temperley makes a half-hearted attempt to punch the ball away. It drops to Dvorski, who has no trouble blasting it home.

Keira jogged back to the centre with a smile on her face. As captain of the first team, she might be worried about Tom Larsson, but today she was also captain of the attacking side, and she was never happier than when her team was winning.

"Marcel never told me that he doesn't get on with Jack," Roddy told Geno, once they were both ready to kick off again.

"Maybe not," said Geno. "But yesterday he told me that he asked to be moved last term. Only Mr Clutterbuck said there are no spare beds. Poor Marcel's got Brett Wilson and Andy Thirwell in his room, too. Sharing with those three would make *anyone* miserable."

"That's tough," said Roddy. "I wish there was something we could do to help."

He looked over to the goal again, where Marcel was standing with his arms hanging limply by his sides. The goalie was filthy from the dives he'd been making, and looked seriously hacked off.

Marek stood a little closer to join in the conversation while they waited for the ball to get back to the centre circle.

"I hope Marcel is more up for it next week," he said. "We've got a house match against Stiles."

On the Spot

Most of Roddy's friends were in Charlton House, and they could see their healthy lead in the competition disappearing without a motivated goalkeeper.

Roddy groaned. "Oh no! That means we're going to be playing against Jack. I bet he tries to wind Marcel up."

"I bet he tries to wind us *all* up," said Marek.

"We mustn't let him get to us," said Geno. "We're a better team than Stiles. If we keep our concentration, we can win easily, *and* keep ahead of Moore and Banks as well."

"All we need is a happy goalie," observed Marek gloomily.

⚽ ⚽ ⚽

During tea that night, Roddy was still thinking about Marcel. Maybe if they went to see Mr Clutterbuck together, it would help. Surely he'd understand how important it was for Marcel to move rooms? Perhaps they could even squeeze another bed in the room Roddy shared with Marek, Geno and Jimmy if it came to it.

Roddy noticed Marcel get up to leave the dining room, and decided to have a quiet word. Charlton couldn't have an off-form goalie just because he was finding life tough. Even though they weren't close friends, Roddy wanted to help if he possibly could. Anything was worth trying if it meant the team would play better.

"See you later," he told Geno.

Geno waved vaguely with his fork. It was pasta, his favourite, and he wasn't about to hurry.

Roddy caught up with Marcel outside, and fell into step with him.

"I'm sorry life's a pain at the moment," he said. "You've got a double whammy, what with Roberts and having to share with those three."

Marcel shrugged. "Brett and Andy aren't so bad when they're not with Jack," he said.

"Well, if you want to try and move rooms again, I'll go with you to see Mr Clutterbuck," Roddy offered awkwardly.

Marcel looked at him in surprise. "What good would that do?" he asked. "He's already told me there's nowhere to go."

Now it was Roddy's turn to shrug. "We could suggest putting an extra bed in our room."

"Clutterbuck's not going to do that!" said Marcel. "There'd hardly be any floor space."

"Well, there must be *something* we can do," said Roddy, trying to think. "We can still go and see him – explain what a pain Jack is. He'll do something when he realises."

"No," said Marcel. "It doesn't matter."

"It *does*," insisted Roddy. "We're both in the same house. We play for the same team. Charltonites should stick together."

Marcel stopped walking. "No," he said flatly. "It really *doesn't* matter."

"But..." Roddy spread his arms wide. "I want to help!"

"It's too late," said Marcel. He looked round to see if anyone was listening. "I don't want this to get out. Promise you won't say anything?"

"Of course," said Roddy. "What is it?"

"I'm leaving on Friday," said Marcel. "My parents are coming to pick me up."

Roddy stared. He couldn't believe his ears. Marcel was leaving Stadium School at the end of the first week of term!

"It's not just Jack," said Marcel, seeing Roddy's expression. "I'm not sure I'm cut out to be a professional footballer after all. I miss

On the Spot

my family and, oh, lots of things. I don't even like the food very much."

"I can't believe it!" said Roddy.

Marcel looked fierce. "Don't say anything to *anyone*. If this gets out, people will go on and on about it, and Jack will make my last two nights an absolute misery. I mean it. If you tell anyone, I'll *kill* you."

"Don't worry," said Roddy. "I'll keep it to myself. But ... I'm sorry you're going."

"Yeah, well, I don't see my future spending hours in the shower cleaning mud off myself," said Marcel. "I really enjoyed football when it was just a game, but here it's too serious. There's more to life, you know?" He smiled sadly. "But that's just what *I* think. You're seriously good. So stick at it. And maybe I'll come and see you some time, when you're playing an international against France, and I'm working in an office or something."

Roddy chuckled. "Yeah, right," he said. "Here's hoping."

Just then, Marek and Jimmy appeared round the corner of the building.

"Don't forget," Marcel warned.

"Don't worry," said Roddy. "You can count on me."

Marcel hurried away and Roddy waited for his friends to catch him up.

"What did Marcel want?" asked Jimmy, dribbling a loose stone along the path.

"Oh, nothing," Roddy said. "He was just telling me how he doesn't like pasta very much."

Marek looked as if he was going to laugh, but the expression on Roddy's face stopped him. "What's the matter?"

Roddy tried to shrug it off, but his mind was working overtime. Now, suddenly, he realised that they wouldn't just have an

On the Spot

off-form goalie for the match against Stiles next week. It was worse than that, much worse. This time next week, they wouldn't have a goalie at all.

2. Desperate Measures

It was terrible for Roddy, not being able to discuss what he knew with his Charlton team-mates, especially Keira. As their captain, she would be appalled when she found out. Stadium School was small, and it was hard enough trying to muster full house teams without a vital student leaving. Roddy wondered what Sam, the senior who coached their team, would do.

Roddy's head was filled with Charlton's goalkeeping problem every spare minute. On his way to French the next day, he considered the backs. Would one of them be any good in goal? Jimmy had the size, but he wasn't very agile, and Jess was lacking in height, if not

On the Spot

courage. Besides, if either of those two became goalie, the team would miss their brilliant defending. The Charlton match against Stiles was the following Saturday, but there was hardly time to sort anything out. First-team training took precedence over house practices, and Mr Jenkins was scheduling extra sessions to get them ready for their first match against Leeds in just over five weeks' time.

In order to help the squad gel, that afternoon Mr Jenkins led them all on a jog around the lake. Despite the chilly weather, it was good to be running somewhere other than round the pitches for a change. Roddy and Geno were jogging steadily near the back of the group and, as they passed a puddle side by side, Geno deliberately stamped into the water, sending a jet shooting up Roddy's leg. Geno flashed a cheeky grin at his friend, before putting his head down and setting off at full speed, with an indignant Roddy in hot pursuit.

Marcel had been running alone, just behind the pair, panting a little. As a goalkeeper, he wasn't used to running for more than a couple of minutes during matches. He had just dropped his pace, when Jack Carr barged past him, sending him staggering towards the muddy edge of the lake. Unlike Geno, who had been fooling around, Jack had clearly meant to upset the French boy.

Marcel squelched out of the mud and resumed his half-hearted run at the back of the squad as Jack sprinted off, laughing.

⚽ ⚽ ⚽

Marcel managed to keep his secret until the Friday afternoon, when he began to pack. It was Jack who found him, stuffing the last of

On the Spot

his belongings into a suitcase. Roddy's heart sank as he heard the bully crashing along the corridor, shouting the news to each room.

Geno looked up from his book. "What is that idiot on about now? We don't care about his latest scandal."

The next moment, Jack burst in, flinging the door open so hard that it hit the wall. "Guess what!" he shouted. "Temperley is running away from school!"

Marek looked at him disapprovingly. "Not interested," he said.

Jack laughed. "Well, you *should* be," he said. "What's your precious Charlton team going to do without a goalie?"

That got Marek's attention, and Geno's and Jimmy's as well.

"What are you on about?" said Jimmy, looking alarmed.

"Poor little Marcel is too much of a baby

to cope," said Jack nastily. "So he's running away! Honestly. He's packed up all his stuff. How spineless is that? He's leaving his team-mates in the lurch! Not that I care..."

"He's *not* running away," said Roddy quietly. "His parents are coming to collect him. It's all arranged."

Now everyone was staring at Roddy.

"You *knew*?" said Jimmy. "You should have told us. We've got a match next week. Sam will need to sort out who to put in goal!"

"You should have told us," said Geno angrily.

"I couldn't!" said Roddy. "Marcel made me promise not to."

Jack was still there, taking it all in, and clearly loving every minute.

"Clear off, Carr!" said Marek angrily. "This is nothing to do with you." He pushed

On the Spot

Jack out of the door and slammed it shut. "Now," he said, turning to Roddy. "What's going on?"

Roddy aimed a kick at the leg of his bed in frustration. "It's not *my* fault," he said. "Now it's out in the open, instead of blaming me, why don't we go and find Sam. As our coach, she's the one who really needs to know."

"Couldn't you have persuaded Marcel to stay?" said Jimmy. "It's going to be hell defending with no goalie."

Roddy gave him a withering look.

Geno fished under his bed for his trainers, and started to put them on. "Roddy's right," he said. "We need to tell Sam."

The four friends hurried over to the girls' boarding house. Sam could be anywhere on a Friday, now lessons had finished, but maybe someone would know where she was.

Roddy rang the bell, and they waited

impatiently. But they were in luck. The girl who answered the door told them that Sam was in, and after a few minutes, their coach came out to see them.

"What's the problem?" she asked.

"We're in deep trouble," Roddy told her gloomily. "Our goalie's doing a bunk."

"No way!" said Sam. "Hang on, I'll just go and get Keira. She needs to be in on this."

Moments later, Sam reappeared with the Charlton captain in tow, and the girls listened as Roddy explained what had happened.

"That certainly is bad news," Sam agreed. "But we mustn't let it throw us."

"It's a *disaster*!" said Geno.

"Where are we going to get another goalie from?" said Keira. "We've only got just enough players as it is."

"I tell you what," Sam decided. "Tomorrow we'll get the whole team

On the Spot

together, and everyone can try out for goalie. You never know, we might find a multi-talented player in our ranks."

"Yeah, right," muttered Jimmy.

"It's the best we can do," said Sam. "It's always tricky finding enough players for inter-house games, but I'm sure we'll find *someone* to go in goal. Besides, we're a stronger team than Stiles, we ought to win the match easily. We'll just have to make sure we don't give our keeper too much to do, whoever they are." She smiled. "Cheer up, all of you. These things happen in football. It's a test of character. We'll manage somehow."

The boys nodded, and Keira looked determined. "Charlton for ever!" she said firmly. "Don't let's lose heart."

⚽ ⚽ ⚽

In the morning, Mr Clutterbuck announced that every Charlton first year was to meet on the practice pitch at two o'clock. Word had spread that Marcel had left, and everyone was wondering how the house would manage without him.

"Hard luck losing Marcel," said Dij, who was in Banks House. "I hope you find a good replacement."

Jack was less sympathetic. "We're going to trash you next Saturday," he crowed.

"Leave it," said Roddy, pulling Jimmy away. "You know Jack would just love it if you started a fight."

Jimmy shook him off. "Let's go then," he growled angrily.

Over at the pitch, most of the girls were there already.

Ashanti came up to Roddy straight away. "This is terrible," she said. "Keira told me last night. And now the whole school knows, what with Jack shooting his great mouth off

On the Spot

at breakfast. Marcel has really gone, has he? He didn't even say goodbye!"

"He left last night," Roddy told her. "He'd kept it quiet, so Jack wouldn't give him any aggro about it. I think he just wanted to disappear, once he'd made his mind up."

"It's a shame," said Keira. "He was a good goalkeeper."

Before they could say anything else, Sam appeared. "OK you lot," she said briskly. "You all know by now that we've lost our goalie. So we'd better find another one. I'm going to put you all in goal. No exceptions. And we'll see who comes out best. The one who does will be our keeper next Saturday against Stiles. Once that hurdle is over, we can take a longer look at the situation. I think Moore have got an extra goalie in your year, and we might be able to get him transferred to Charlton."

Desperate Measures

"But they'll need him while Tom Larsson's injured," Roddy pointed out. "Couldn't we have Glen Hardcastle on loan?"

Everybody laughed. Glen Hardcastle was the goalkeeper for Charlton senior boys. In fact, he was the best goalkeeper Stadium School had.

"That would show Jack," said Geno with a grin. "I'd *love* to do something to wipe the smug expression off his face."

"Unfortunately, Roddy, you have to be a first year to play in a first-year team," laughed Sam. "But that's the spirit. Don't let this problem get you down. We'll find a solution if we put our minds to it. Now, let's find our new goalie!"

3. A Big Surprise

"Any volunteers?" said Sam.

There was plenty of muttering, but nobody put themselves forward.

"OK, then. We'll start with a penalty shootout," said Sam. "I'll take five shots against each of you, and everyone who saves one will go on to the next test."

Keira went first, but she had no chance. Sam had a fierce left foot, and she wasn't going to make things easy.

"I'm just not cut out for the job," Keira said, as she picked the fifth ball out of the net. "You next, Roddy."

Roddy tried his best, but he was just as bad as Keira. He was too short to be a keeper.

A Big Surprise

Every shot was too far away for him to reach. Jess surprised herself by getting a hand to one shot, and Stephen Mbeki managed to pull off a save, too. Eboni and Ashanti didn't make any real effort, and it was obvious that they didn't want the job. Finally, Marek was the only one left. He'd been avoiding the goalie gloves as if they had some horrible disease, but Sam insisted that everyone had to try.

Reluctantly, Marek went to stand between the posts.

And the pressure is really on the rookie goalkeeper today. Green, an experienced and composed taker of penalties, will be looking to get all five of these past Dvorski, who is only in goal today as an emergency measure. She begins her run-up, and cracks the ball firmly into the back of the net. Dvorski didn't even come close to that one, and wordlessly

On the Spot

rolls the ball back to Green. She steps back, and sends the ball skidding across the wet grass towards the bottom corner. Dvorski guesses right, and manages to get his fingertips to the ball. But it's not enough, and the ball squirms past him into the goal. Two from two so far for Green.

"Unlucky, Marek, you nearly had that one!" said Sam encouragingly.

Marek just nodded, but it seemed to Roddy that he was now standing more purposefully in the goal. Crouched down with his gloves out ready to stop the ball, he cut an imposing figure, and Roddy fancied his chances.

Third penalty now, and Dvorski is growing in confidence. Green halts her run-up before the ball this time, trying to con the keeper into diving early, but he sees through her trick. Put off by her own gambit, she knocks

A Big Surprise

a tame shot at waist height and Dvorski pulls off an easy save. His team applaud; the stand-in goalie could be a hero today.

Sam looked disgusted at her own effort, but congratulated Marek. Again, he took her comments silently and just waited for the next shot. He still had two chances to save another shot, a feat no one else had accomplished.

Dvorski must be buzzing after that last save, and Green knows that she can't play games. She hits her fourth shot straight into the top-right corner, leaving the keeper no chance. Nobody could have saved that, and Dvorski knows it. He returns the ball for the final time, and begins to try some mind games with the striker. He stands slightly off-centre in the goalmouth, leaving one side of the goal wider than the other and giving Green a dilemma. Dvorski will be expecting

On the Spot

her to shoot for the space, so she should aim for where he is standing. On the other hand, it could be a double bluff. She takes a deep breath, runs up to the ball and hammers it straight at where Dvorski is standing. The keeper has begun to dive to his right, but realises his mistake and trails his legs through the air. The ball thuds into his shins and bounces clear of the goal. What a save!

Sam shook off the disappointment of missing two penalties.

"Well done, Marek, that was a brilliant, instinctive save. You looked like a natural-born goalie. Well done to everyone else, too, you mostly gave it your best, and that's what the Charlton spirit is all about. Now, Marek, Stephen and Jess, can you three stay a little longer, please. Everyone else is free to go."

As Roddy, Geno and Jimmy wandered back to the boarding house, the talk was all about Marek's goalkeeping talents. "Do you think he's the best?" asked Geno.

"None of the others are really tall enough," replied Roddy. "I mean, they're a normal height, but Marek is a giant. It's a massive advantage."

"And he did save two penalties." Geno pointed out. "Nearly three."

"Remember when we first met him, though," said Jimmy. "I said he should be a goalie and he almost bit my head off. I hope he can deal with the decision if he really is our best chance."

"I guess we'll just have to wait and see," said Roddy.

⊕ ⊕ ⊕

It was almost dark by the time Marek crashed into the common room and flopped on to a sofa, still wearing his muddy kit. He was immediately surrounded by Charlton juniors

On the Spot

asking questions, but he just shut his eyes and waved them away.

Only Geno persisted. "Just tell us if you got it."

Marek sighed. "I'm very tired. Sam kept me there for hours, teaching me how to be a goalkeeper. She thinks I'm the answer to our problem for now. *That's it*," he said loudly, before he could be interrupted. "And now I'm going for a shower."

4. A Nail-biting Match

The match against Stiles came round quickly and Marek had little time to practise in goal. Sam had done her best to get Marek up to speed, but today was going to require mostly natural skill and a big dollop of luck.

"This is going to be much tougher than last time you played Stiles," she said, as the team prepared to take the field. "They were without Jack then. He'll have told his players to get plenty of attempts at goal. Marek, look out for them trying long shots all the time. Just stay alert. If they get in close, remember what I taught you about closing down the angles. With your height, they shouldn't be able to chip you, so they'll have

On the Spot

to go round. Everyone else, just tr

on to possession if you possibly c

nothing wrong with passing back

means we keep the ball. It may sou

but if they haven't got the ball,

score. So, good luck. But I hope

need it. After all, we're a stronger t

Keira added her own quick

encouragement, and then spent

minute talking to Marek. He looked

in the goalie's kit, uncomfortable

ways, but he certainly had the bu

the multi-coloured shirt.

It's Charlton versus Stiles here to

the big news is that the Polish strike

Dvorski, is playing in goal for c

Charlton will play one up front to

four in defence instead of their cu

three. They'll be trying to stifle

creative players with a 4–5–1 forma t

4. A Nail-biting Match

The match against Stiles came round quickly and Marek had little time to practise in goal. Sam had done her best to get Marek up to speed, but today was going to require mostly natural skill and a big dollop of luck.

"This is going to be much tougher than last time you played Stiles," she said, as the team prepared to take the field. "They were without Jack then. He'll have told his players to get plenty of attempts at goal. Marek, look out for them trying long shots all the time. Just stay alert. If they get in close, remember what I taught you about closing down the angles. With your height, they shouldn't be able to chip you, so they'll have to go round. Everyone else, just try and hang on to possession if you possibly can. There's nothing wrong with passing backwards if it means we keep the ball. It may sound obvious, but if they haven't got the ball, they can't score. So, good luck. But I hope you won't need it. After all, we're a stronger team."

Keira added her own quick words of encouragement, and then spent an extra minute talking to Marek. He looked different in the goalie's kit, uncomfortable in some ways, but he certainly had the build to fill the multi-coloured shirt.

It's Charlton versus Stiles here today, and the big news is that the Polish striker, Marek Dvorski, is playing in goal for Charlton. Charlton will play one up front today, and four in defence instead of their customary three. They'll be trying to stifle Stiles' creative players with a 4–5–1 formation, and

A Nail-biting Match

looking to give Dvorski as little work to do as possible. Perotti is going to have a tough time of it as a lone striker, so Jones and Sanders will need to support him as much as they can.

The whistle blows, and Stiles kick off. The Charlton midfield gets to work straight away, trying to break up any attempt to play the ball forward. Stiles find a way up the pitch, though, and take a long shot at goal. It's on target but tame, and Dvorski collects it with relative ease. He's passed the first test, but he'll have a lot more to worry about as the game goes on.

"Well done, Marek. Keep it up," said Roddy as he got within earshot of the keeper. Marek raised a glove in acknowledgement, then returned to watching the ball intently. If he did let in any goals today, it wouldn't be from lack of concentration.

On the Spot

Charlton have the ball now, but it seems that they're more worried about keeping possession than scoring a goal themselves. Sanders, Jones and Mbeki are playing neat triangles in the middle of the pitch, just letting the clock tick. The Nagel twins are on the wings, looking for an opportunity to break... and now it looks like they've found one! Jones launches a long pass up the left-hand side, and Eboni Nagel gives chase. She reaches the ball a split second before the Stiles full-back, and hits a cross into the box without having time to aim properly. The ball flies over Perotti's head and is easily cleared by the centre back. Dvorski would have got to that cross, but Charlton will just have to learn to cope without his size up front.

The loose ball is picked up by Carr in midfield, and the Stiles captain lopes forward into the Charlton half. He passes the ball away but is immediately calling for the return pass. He gets it, and unleashes a piledriver from outside the area. Dvorski gets behind the ball, but spills it into the path of the Stiles striker, who slots it home. 1–0 to Stiles, and Dvorski won't want to dwell on that mistake. A more experienced keeper might have pushed it clear. Carr is celebrating right in the face of the Charlton keeper, and the ref's not too pleased. He takes Carr to one side, then shows him a yellow card for unsporting behaviour.

Jack trudged back to the halfway line, grumbling to himself as he walked. Roddy was glad to see him carded, but they were still a goal down. Sam was behind the goalposts, quickly giving Marek a bit more advice, but half-time was approaching. If they could keep the Stiles lead to one goal, they'd still have a chance in the second half.

On the Spot

Stiles have a free kick in a dangerous area, and you'd put money on them shooting from there. Dvorski arranges his defensive wall, then crouches in anticipation.

Roddy could see the concentration on Marek's face. Matt Barker, the Stiles player taking the free kick, began his run-up, and Roddy crossed his fingers.

It's a scorching shot from Barker, but Dvorski makes a great save! He got down well to his left and held on to the ball.

Roddy grinned widely as the whistle blew. He joined Jimmy and Marek as they came off the field and added his congratulations to the rookie keeper as they went into the team-talk room.

"We're a goal down, but you're doing a great job, Marek," Sam began. "We were unlucky to concede the first one, but that save just now was fantastic!" Marek looked pleased. "It's been tight so far defensively," she went on. "But we're struggling going forward. Geno doesn't have Marek's height, so we can't cross the ball in like we used to. We need to keep it on the ground and use his pace. Eboni and Ashanti, swap sides in the second half. I want you both cutting in and shooting rather than crossing. Got that?"

"Yes, Sam," the twins chorused.

"Good. Roddy and Keira, you two should be pushing up whenever we've got the ball. Three people in the box will worry them a lot more than just Geno on his own. Four defenders plus Stephen should be able to cope with the Stiles attack, so let's get up their end and make a game of it!"

The Charlton team have come on to the pitch looking fired up. From the kickoff, they're looking to get the ball forward. Sanders passes the ball out right to Ashanti...

On the Spot

no, it's Eboni Nagel, they've swapped sides. Nagel runs at the full-back, who is expecting her to make for the by-line, but instead she cuts inside leaving him completely wrong-footed. She bursts into the penalty area, drawing the keeper towards her, then plays a simple ball square to Perotti, who calmly pushes it into an open goal. Game on.

Sam cheered from the touchline. Her plan had paid dividends right away. "Brilliant," she said. "Let's have another one of those!"

Stiles kick off, and their captain is raging at his players. It certainly seems to be motivating them, as Charlton are being held in their own half again, and their goal is peppered with long-range shots. Dvorski is coping well so far, but the pressure is unrelenting. He makes another excellent save, tipping the ball over the bar for a corner.

A Nail-biting Match

Roddy had seen Mr Jenkins arrive soon after the second half began, accompanied by the senior captains. He knew that it was vital to be seen playing well, in order to secure a place in the starting eleven for the first team's match against Leeds. It was still almost four weeks until the game, and Roddy didn't want to be left on the bench.

Piper heads the corner clear, and the ball is picked up by Jones. With so many players forward, Stiles have left big gaps in defence, and that's exactly what the young Welsh-Brazilian thrives on. He pushes the ball forward, and leaves everyone else for dead with his pace. Carr is there ahead of him and, as Jones tries to get past, his shirt is tugged by the Stiles captain. Jones tries to play on, but the ref has blown for a free kick. He's summoned Carr over to him, and it's his second yellow card! Jack Carr has been sent

On the Spot

off, and Stiles will play the rest of the game with ten men. It's an early bath for the Stiles captain!

Roddy was relieved to see Jack leaving the pitch. He'd been getting more and more angry, and Roddy counted himself lucky that he'd only had his shirt pulled. It could have been much worse. Now, Charlton had the advantage.

Stephen Mbeki, Charlton's defensive midfielder takes the free kick and plays it short to Sanders, who passes it to Jones. Jones knocks the ball up to Perotti, who does well to hold off two defenders and play it back towards Jones. Jones runs on to the ball and drives a low shot in from the edge of the area. The keeper dives for it, but the ball slides under his body and into the back of the net. 2–1 to Charlton!

Roddy glanced at Mr Jenkins, who was

A Nail-biting Match

standing on the touchline. He was talking to David, the Charlton House captain, but was it about Roddy, or just the match? Roddy put it to the back of his mind, and went back to his own half for the kickoff.

Charlton will want to sit tight and hold on to the win. Going for another goal isn't worth the risk and, with the minutes ticking away, they'll fancy their chances of keeping ten-man Stiles out. They're getting everyone behind the ball to try and keep defence tight, and it appears to be working.

Chris Wood, the Stiles midfielder, hits a screamer of a shot in from long range, but Dvorski is equal to it and makes another magnificent save. He's really kept Charlton in the game today. You wouldn't believe it's his first match playing in goal. Dvorski hoofs it down the pitch, the ref checks his watch and it's all over. Charlton have turned it round in

On the Spot

the second half and won the game. Stiles will feel let down by their captain, but credit has to go to Charlton for a bold performance.

The Charlton players all gathered round Marek, showering him with praise. The stand-in keeper tried to brush off the attention, but he was definitely the hero of the hour.

"You were brilliant," said Roddy, slapping Marek on his back.

"But *you* scored the winning goal." replied Marek. "*I* was only the keeper."

5. A Big Shock

Roddy and Marek were up early on Monday morning, and even beat Mr Jenkins onto the field for their training session.

"Fancy taking a few shots on goal while we're waiting?" said Marek. "I'll try saving them, if you like."

"You're really getting into your keeping, aren't you?" said Roddy, as they made their way to the closest set of posts.

"It's fun!" laughed Marek. "I'm not sure it beats *scoring* goals, but it's great being the last line of defence and pulling off a good save. I didn't think I would, but I really enjoyed the match on Saturday. And Jack's face was hilarious when he was sent off."

Long Shot

Roddy sent a scorcher of a ball towards Marek, who fell on his knees to capture it. "You'll have to do better than that," he laughed triumphantly, throwing the ball back.

"Let's have a go," said Keira, who had just arrived with the twins.

"All right. Headers and volleys," replied Roddy, chipping the ball towards Eboni.

Eboni ran to meet the ball and smashed it goalwards with her left foot, but Marek pulled off another stunning save.

As more of the year arrived, a game developed, and everyone was a little disappointed when Mr Jenkins arrived and set them to doing proper training drills. Not so long ago, Roddy would have struggled to play an energetic game then do a training session afterwards, but Mr Jenkins's emphasis on fitness and stamina was really working.

A Big Shock

Roddy's times for running laps of the pitch were getting better and better, and the cool January sunshine kept him at a comfortable temperature as he ran.

On the way to the changing rooms after the practice session, Mr Jenkins cornered Marek. By the time he got under the shower, everyone else was changed, but his friends were waiting for him in the team-talk room.

"What did Mr Jenkins want?" asked Roddy, when Marek appeared.

"You're not going to believe this," said Marek. "He reckons I ought to consider training as a goalie for the first team."

"Really?" Keira thought about it. "Well, you do seem to have the talent for it."

"I'm helping out Charlton, and that's fine, but I don't want to be a goalie for ever," said Marek.

"But you're so good at it!" said Jimmy.

On the Spot

"That's not the point!" said Marek. He glared at Jimmy. "I'm a striker, aren't I? I'm not going to abandon that. I've always wanted to be a striker, and that's what I'm going to be when I turn professional."

"OK, OK," laughed Jimmy, lifting his hands. "Don't blow your top. Everyone knows you're a striker. So what did you say?"

"I reminded him that I was a striker," Marek said seriously.

"Oh, Marek, really. You *are* an idiot," laughed Geno. "You did so well in the House Cup match, *and* you've got the height. You should go for it."

"You're only saying that because you're a striker, like me." Marek sounded cross. "You want the glory of scoring all the goals with me out of the way."

Geno looked shocked. "No way," he insisted. "I'd love to be more of an all-rounder. And goalkeepers are always in demand. Any team would be pleased to have someone in the squad who plays up front, but is also handy as a keeper. It wouldn't have to be your main position."

"But that's the problem!" said Marek. "The school's got plenty of forwards and a shortage of keepers, and I think Mr Jenkins wants me to sacrifice my career as a striker and be a goalie full time!" Then he gathered his kit and stomped off.

Roddy and Geno exchanged glances. "He'd probably get on well with Mr Roberts," said Geno. "They've both had a sense-of-humour bypass!"

"He does take things very seriously," agreed Keira. "You'd think he'd have been flattered that Mr Jenkins even suggested it."

For the next few days, Marek kept well away from goal while Mr Jenkins was

On the Spot

around, but Roddy noticed that he was still enjoying keeping for Sam at the Charlton House training sessions. And they had a tough match against Moore coming up in less than two weeks, so it was just as well. Despite their healthy lead over the other first-year teams, Charlton was behind Moore in the competition overall. Moore had won the House Cup last year, but this time things were so tight that every goal counted.

⚽ ⚽ ⚽

A couple of days later, before training, Mr Jenkins cornered Marek as he and Roddy emerged from the changing rooms.

"Hang on a minute, Marek, can I have a word?" he said. "I'd like you to have a short session with Mr Roberts today."

Marek stopped dead. Roddy could see him working himself up to an angry reply, but Mr Jenkins got there first.

A Big Shock

"I know you keep saying that you don't have any ambition to be a goalkeeper," he said. "But you're currently playing that position in the House Cup. All the other goalies get special training, and Charlton shouldn't miss out. You might find you pick up some useful tips."

Marek opened his mouth and then shut it again. He still hadn't managed to say anything by the time Mr Jenkins walked away.

Roddy nudged him in the ribs. "Come on then, *goalie*," he teased. "Where's your multi-coloured shirt?"

"Shut up," said Marek. "I'm not a goalkeeper. I'm..."

"You need it tattooed on your forehead, so people don't forget," Roddy said. He lifted his hand and began to trace the letters on his friends head. "S... T... R... I..."

"Get off!" snarled Marek.

On the Spot

⚽ ⚽ ⚽

After their run, Marek did as he was told and trained with Mr Roberts. When he finally came over to join everyone, he was looking rather muddy, but quite content.

"How'd it go?" asked Roddy.

Marek's mood changed immediately. He looked suspiciously at Roddy before admitting, "OK." Then he jogged over to Stephen Mbeki and started talking to him.

Roddy shrugged and went to see Keira.

"What's up with him?" she asked.

Roddy frowned. "I made the mistake of teasing him about being a goalkeeper, and he didn't like it," he said.

"Well, mind you don't upset him," she warned. "We need him happy and in top form for our match against Moore."

"Don't worry," said Roddy. "He'll come round." Then they both went their separate ways to shower and change before the normal school day took over.

⚽ ⚽ ⚽

After training that afternoon, they had some free time, and Roddy challenged Jimmy to a game of pool. They were about to set off back to their boarding house when Roddy paused. "Have you seen Marek?" he asked, wondering if he wanted to play pool, too.

"He's over there, look." Jimmy pointed to the field.

He was right. Marek hadn't gone in like everyone else. He was still out practising his shooting skills, with a half-empty net of balls by his feet. Time after time, he would spot a ball, take a run up, and aim for the goal.

Roddy watched for a few moments. Marek was really pushing himself. He was obviously trying to reach the top-right corner of the net. He got a couple on target, but several

On the Spot

times he hit the woodwork, and a few shots missed entirely. It was going to be a pain collecting up all the balls again. For a moment, Roddy thought about offering to help. But he'd just had a shower, and got changed. It was a chilly day and he was looking forward to his game of pool.

"Leave him to it," urged Jimmy. "He'll come in when he's had enough."

"I suppose," agreed Roddy. "But what's he doing it for? He doesn't usually spend extra time out there."

There was something strange going on, and Roddy was determined to get to the bottom of it.

6. Marek Owns Up

At weekends, some people went out for the day with parents or relations. Roddy's family lived too far away for that, so he always stayed in school, but on the next Sunday, Marek was collected by his cousin. When he came back, he was grinning.

"Look at this!" he said, coming into the common room and unrolling a large, Polish flag. "My cousin got it for me. I hope I can watch the match on TV tonight. It's a big game for my country."

"Great!" said Roddy enthusiastically. "Let's hang up the flag somewhere in here."

"Did you have a nice time with your cousin?" asked Geno.

On the Spot

"Yes," said Marek. "His wife cooked a Polish meal, and it was delicious. Much better than English food."

Gino noticed the look on his face and laughed. "I think you just made a joke," he said.

"Maybe," said Marek, with a slight smile.

There was a good crowd to watch Poland's match against Latvia, and most people were supporting Marek's country. Mr Clutterbuck came in to watch the second half, and there was a nail-biting finish. A huge groan went up from everyone when Poland gave away a penalty, but the shot went wide, and they just managed to pull off a win.

"Is your cousin keen on football?" asked Roddy, as they went upstairs to bed.

Marek spread the flag over his duvet before getting in. "Oh, yes!" he said. "In fact..." he paused, and looked serious. "He says he's coming to watch me play in the match against Leeds."

"Lucky you," said Roddy enthusiastically.

"You'll have to make sure you get your place in the starting line-up, then," said Jimmy.

"As if Marek needs to worry about that," said Geno. "He's been doing extra training all week, practising free kicks and penalties."

"But I've been training with Mr Roberts, too," Marek said. "So there's been less time to spend on my *proper* training."

"You worry too much," said Geno sleepily.

Marek turned over and the bed creaked. "You know how tough it is to get picked for the first team," he said. "If I let my game suffer, Mr Jenkins will drop me, and my cousin is expecting to see me shine."

"I suppose, if the worst happened and you did get dropped, you could always invite

On the Spot

your cousin to see you play in a Charlton match," Roddy suggested.

Marek looked at him in horror. "I couldn't do that!" he said. "I'd be playing in the wrong position. I can't let him see me being a goalkeeper!"

"Why not?" asked Jimmy.

Marek sat up and took a deep breath. "When I was very young, my father took me to watch Poland play," he told them. "My hero had always been Maciej Żurawski. He had a great game, and afterwards I went round to the players' entrance so I could ask for his autograph."

"I've done that at Villa Park," said Jimmy.

Marek glared at him, and Jimmy fell silent. Żurawski was so kind to me," continued Marek. "He stopped to talk, and asked me what my ambition was. When I admitted that I wanted to be a striker like him, he said

I could be if I wanted to. If I tried hard enough." Marek looked seriously at his friends. "I believed him. And I still believe him. All my family have known of my ambition for years. What would they think if my cousin tells them that he saw me not scoring for my side, but sprawled in the mud, trying to save goals instead?" And with that, Marek got out of bed and stomped moodily from the room.

Roddy watched him go and then whistled. "Phew," he said. "That boy has a big problem, doesn't he? Why does it matter what position he plays in? He's turning out to be a great all-rounder. He's really lucky."

"I'd love to be more of an all-rounder," Jimmy agreed. "But it might be really confusing. I mean, what if you forgot you weren't playing in goal and put your hand up for the ball?"

On the Spot

"Some players do change positions," said Roddy, putting his wash bag and towel away. "Peter Schmeichel started out as a striker, then he went on to become one of the best keepers in the world. Loads of people move around the pitch while they're learning, it gives them a better knowledge of the game. You get to know all the tricks of the people you'll be up against, and what they're likely to do."

Marek reappeared and climbed wordlessly into bed. Then Mr Clutterbuck poked his head round the door to check they were all ready to go to sleep.

"Night, lads," he said, turning off the light.

Roddy let Mr Clutterbuck's footsteps fade away down the corridor before he spoke. "We've got a tough match against Moore on Saturday, but we can do it. Charlton for ever!"

Marek Owns Up

"Charlton for ever," came the mumbled
reply.

7. A Difficult Time

The term was moving on. Four weeks had already passed, but there was a lot to look forward to. The match against Leeds was looming large on the horizon, and provided a target for everyone to work towards.

Today, however, all thoughts were on the House Cup. Charlton first years were playing Moore in the afternoon.

After morning training, it was IT, one of Roddy's least favourite subjects. However, Mr Davies, the teacher, tried to make the lesson interesting by giving them a football-related exercise to do.

"You're all chairmen of your favourite clubs," he told them, writing busily on the whiteboard. "We're going to look at how you can use spreadsheets to keep track of your budget. Now, let's have a few ideas of things you'll need to buy."

The suggestions were quick to come, and Roddy was enjoying himself.

"Players!" was the first suggestion.

"Staff. Maintenance. Electricity?"

"Good," said Mr Davies. "And how are you going to get money in to pay for all this?"

"Tickets!"

"Sponsorship!"

"TV money!"

Soon Mr Davies had introduced the class to simple spreadsheets, and they had a long list of items to budget for. This wasn't quite so much fun, and Roddy's head started to spin. He glanced out of the window, and saw a class of older students out on one of the

On the Spot

practice pitches, playing a match. He wished he were there, too, instead of stuck indoors with a load of figures.

And Jones has the ball at his feet. He's surrounded by players much older and stronger than him, but his magical skills are letting him run rings around them all. He beats one man ... two ... three, and he's one on one with the keeper. Roddy Jones draws back his foot to shoot and...

"Roddy Jones!"

Roddy jumped, and turned away from the window.

"If I catch you daydreaming again, I'll dock you some house points," Mr Davies threatened.

Roddy saw several Charltonites glaring, and he gave them an apologetic grin. He focussed on the spreadsheet again, but however hard he tried, he just couldn't get his budget to balance. To raise enough money, he'd have to sell his best player, but if he did that he might not get so many people in to watch the matches, and then his income would go down, and he'd be broke again, with a weaker team as well. Roddy groaned. Whatever he did with his life, he must remember never to take on the job of chairman of a football club!

⚽ ⚽ ⚽

After lunch, it was a relief to get outside for the match. A cold wind was sweeping across the field, but even so, lots of students had turned out to watch.

Keira assembled her team for a pre-match pep talk. "We need to play our best attacking game to have a chance of winning," she reminded them. "Moore are strong in every position and we can't win by sitting back and defending. We learned that against Stiles.

Long Shot

It's far better to draw 4–4 than lose 1–0.
Football's about scoring goals, not worrying
so much about conceding that you never
attack. And with Marcel Temperley and Tom
Larsson both out of the picture, neither team
is playing their first-choice keeper. So just
enjoy yourselves and get stuck in."

*Today's match between Moore and
Charlton is being played in blustery
conditions, and we may have rain later.
Dvorski is in goal again for Charlton. After his
recent heroics against Stiles, the new goalie
may not be the weak spot Moore were
hoping to exploit. The Polish striker has
proved a very capable stand-in keeper, and
Moore need to take him seriously. Charlton
are short of options up front, however, and
Perotti's going to need plenty of support
from midfield if he wants to crack the Moore
defence. Brett Wilson is standing in for the*

injured Tom Larsson as goalie, and no doubt the imposing American will be trying to stake a permanent claim to the number-one shirt.

Moore kick off, and play the ball around in their own half as they settle into the game. The Charlton attackers are hustling them, and trying to force an error. McInnes, in the Moore defence, passes back to the goalie, but there's not enough weight on the pass and it's left stranded. Perotti gets there first. He takes it round the goalie and places the ball in the open net. Wilson has his head in his hands. Charlton have scored an early goal on the break.

Geno couldn't celebrate for long. There was still plenty of time for Moore to come back into the game.

"Good work," encouraged Keira. "You forced the mistake, but they won't roll over for us. We must keep up the effort."

On the Spot

Charlton have taken an early lead, but Moore are starting to look like the stronger team. Dvorski makes a top-class save to deny the Moore striker Finnigan, and is applauded by the supporters. He rolls the ball out to Jess Ponting, the left full-back, who passes it back inside to Mbeki. Mbeki plays it up to Sanders, whose pass to Eboni Nagel is intercepted. Moore are sweeping forward now, and Charlton are in trouble. Finnigan shoots, and although Dvorski gets a hand to it, the rebound is bundled in by Bullard. It was a scrappy goal, but they all count. Moore are back on level terms!

Marek looked disgusted, but Keira told him not to worry. "We'll score another one, just you wait. You're doing brilliantly."

Half-time is approaching, and these two teams are very evenly matched. The whistle blows, and the teams get a few minutes rest from this nail-biting contest.

"Good effort so far," said Sam, once they were all gathered in the team-talk room. "A draw wouldn't be a bad result today, but I think you can win. Keep trying to hit them on the counterattack without exposing yourselves. Marek, you're working extremely hard. Keep it up. If we can score another goal, that should do the trick. They won't get any past you."

The teams return to the field, and Charlton kick off. Jones and Sanders are taking up more advanced positions this half. Charlton look to be going all out for the win here. Moore will struggle to contain Charlton's attacking flair, but it could be dangerous if Charlton leave their defence exposed too often.

Sanders picks up the ball from a Moore goal kick, and feeds it to Jones. Jones plays

On the Spot

it back to Sanders, who moves further up the field. Perotti drops deep to get involved with the move, and slowly but surely the ball is moved towards the Moore goal. This is great play from Charlton, but it needs an end result. The Moore defence are holding firm, and in the end Sanders chances a long shot. It's on target, but the Moore goalie makes a comfortable save. Charlton rush back to their own half to defend again, and the keeper hits it long, into the path of the Moore left winger. This is real end-to-end stuff.

Moore are on the offensive now, and Dvorski is forced to make another good save, tipping a fierce shot from Bullard behind for a corner. Charlton have everyone back in their own area apart from Perotti and, as the ball comes in, Piper gets his head to it. The Charlton attack stream down the pitch. Mbeki knocks it ahead of Jones, who catches up to the ball on the halfway line. He sees the Moore keeper off his line, and tries an audacious long chip. The keeper is back-pedalling frantically, and everyone else is just standing and watching. The ball seems to arc in slow motion, dropping towards the goal. The keeper isn't going to make it in time, but neither is the ball. It bounces off the crossbar and into the relieved arms of the goalie. That's unlucky. Jones is denied a spectacular goal!

A collective groan went up from everyone watching, followed by a smattering of applause from the Charlton supporters. Roddy had been inches away from scoring an amazing goal, but he couldn't dwell on it. There were still a few minutes left to play, plenty of time for either team to score.

Both sides have thrown caution to the wind in an attempt to take the win, but time

On the Spot

is running out. As another Moore attack is thwarted by Charlton's defence, the ref looks at his watch and blows the final whistle. Either team could have won this, but a draw is probably the fairest result. There's been magnificent entertainment here this afternoon.

Both teams came off the field grinning, even though the wind had brought rain with it for the second half of the match.

"Not a bad result!" gasped Roddy to Keira.

"Yeah," agreed Keira, catching her breath. "We had them on the back foot at the start. Geno's early goal really got them rattled. Pity we couldn't keep it up. But they played really well, and their defence is better organised. You almost won it for us, though."

"I know. It was so close," Roddy agreed.

A Difficult Time

"But didn't Marek cope brilliantly."

"He did," said Keira, looking around for her keeper. "Hey, Marek! You played a blinder. Moore had loads of shots on target. It was amazing you only let one in."

Marek joined Keira and Roddy. "I let in one too many," he said. But although he looked tired, and a bruise was coming on from when he'd dived bravely at John Finnigan's feet, he seemed happy. "I really enjoyed the match," he added with a grin.

"Glad to hear it." Keira returned the grin. "But I'm getting cold. It's time for a shower. Coming, girls?" she called to Jess, Ashanti and Eboni, who were coming off the field.

"See you in the team-talk room," said Roddy, as he and Marek headed for their own changing rooms.

After showering, they had a chance to discuss the match in more comfort.

On the Spot

"The senior girls won their last match against Moore, and the senior boys drew," said Roddy. "So in the overall competition, we're catching them up."

"Did you hear some of their comments afterwards?" said Geno. "Moore were claiming they should have had a penalty. What rubbish! They lost fair and square."

"Completely," agreed Jimmy. "But after their senior teams' results, that lot were desperate to beat us today. Plus we're still way ahead of them in the first years' cup."

Roddy got himself a cup of water from the machine feeling extremely satisfied with their performance. And Marek seemed happy, too. As far as Roddy could see, Marek got as much pleasure from goalkeeping as being a striker. And if he could only stop worrying about what his family thought, he'd probably enjoy it even more.

A Difficult Time

The sad thing was, Marek had been out on the pitch for the last two days, doing extra scoring practice, trying to improve his accuracy, and making up for all the time he was spending training as a goalie. But the extra practice didn't seem to be doing him any good. In fact, his performance as a striker was getting worse. Roddy wondered if Mr Jenkins had noticed. He probably had. The junior coach never missed things like that. With the Leeds match coming up in a week and a half, he'd be announcing the team any day now. Even though he was desperate to know, it made Roddy nervous simply thinking about it. But for Marek it must be much worse. He desperately needed to raise his game if he wanted to be included in the starting line-up. And knowing that his cousin was coming to watch would be adding to his stress.

On the Spot

However, at that moment, Marek was giving Ashanti an animated, blow-by-blow account of his saves. Roddy smiled to himself. Sometimes it was difficult to remember that Marek's preferred position involved *scoring* goals.

8. Bad News

The following Wednesday, a week before the game against Leeds, Mr Jenkins called the first years together after their morning training session.

"The whole team's still not set in stone," he said. "I haven't settled on my subs yet, but these are the names I want to see in the starting line-up. Dij Anichebe, Jimmy Piper, George McInnes, David Peters, Toby Harris, Roddy Jones, Keira Sanders, Ali Patel, Matt Barker, Geno Perotti, Eric Bullard."

Roddy heaved a sigh of relief. Lately he'd been quietly confident of getting in, though there had always been enough doubt to keep him anxious. But poor Marek! He glanced

On the Spot

around for his roommate, to give him a sympathetic look, but Marek was standing some distance away, his face and body as still as a rock.

"I have a list of possibles for the bench," went on Mr Jenkins. "But I want you to have a few more days to prove your worth. So all's not lost. I'll announce the subs on Monday. Meanwhile, there'll be a first-squad practice tomorrow afternoon. I want to see you playing together more as a team. Roddy and Keira have the right idea. Unselfishness and co-operation. That's what I want from all of you."

As soon as Mr Jenkins dismissed them, Marek headed off towards the changing rooms. It was obvious that he didn't want to talk. By the time the rest of the boys arrived, Marek was already dressed and ready to leave. But if he'd hoped to escape without any comment, he was disappointed.

"It's not surprising old Jenkins left you out of the team," Jack sneered. "You can't shoot and you can't keep goals out, either. That was an easy save you missed during your last house match! In fact, I don't know what you're doing at this school at all. You're useless all round."

"That's not true, and you know it. Besides, *you* didn't make the starting line-up, either," Roddy pointed out.

Jack flinched. The jibe had obviously hit him hard. But he soon recovered and laughed unpleasantly. "And now you have to get your little friends to stand up for you, too," he snarled. Then he stuffed his hands in his pockets and sauntered off.

Roddy was fuming. Marek gave no hint as to what he was feeling, but he threw on his jacket in a hurry and left for the next lesson.

On the Spot

"I keep thinking that Jack can't be *all* bad, and then he goes and spoils everything," Geno muttered. "How could he *say* something like that? What's Marek ever done to him?"

"Nothing," Roddy replied. "I think he's just jealous because we're such good friends. He hardly has any mates at all."

"It's not surprising, is it?" said Jimmy. "And the people he shares with don't help, either."

"I think Brett and Andy just go along with him to make life easier for themselves," said Roddy. "I didn't used to think so, but when you get them on their own they're all right."

"What are we going to do about Marek?" asked Geno, changing the subject. "He must be really upset about not making the team."

"Let's try to talk to him at lunch," said Roddy, and with that he hurried outside, almost bumping straight into Mr Jenkins.

The coach was talking earnestly to Marek, so Roddy hung around, a few paces away, waiting for them to finish their conversation. He was intrigued to find out what Mr Jenkins was saying this time.

"And I really mean it," Mr Jenkins concluded. "As soon as you relax, the accuracy will come back. You've lost belief in yourself. That's the trouble." Then he patted Marek on his shoulder and hurried away.

Roddy joined Marek, and they walked towards the main house together. For a few moments, neither said anything. Then Marek spoke. "He told me to stop the extra practice," he said miserably.

"Why?" said Roddy, not wanting to admit that he'd overheard anything.

"He says I've overdone it," said Marek.

"Well, maybe he's right," said Roddy.

On the Spot

There was another pause.

Marek's mouth twisted as he struggled with his feelings. "He keeps telling me I ought to concentrate on goalkeeping for a while because, he says, I enjoy it. And he says I have a natural talent for it." Marek stopped walking and turned to look at his friend. "But I'm really scared that he's going to drop me as a striker altogether, and try to get me to be a full-time goalie!"

Roddy sighed. "That wouldn't be so terrible, would it? Maybe that's what you're really cut out for. We're short of good goalies," he added in a rush. "Especially while Tom Larsson is unfit. But there are loads of people who want to play up front."

"That's because it's where the glory is," said Marek. "And anyway." He looked torn. "How can I change my mind? I've never mentioned goalkeeping to my family."

"It's not against the law to change your mind," said Roddy.

Marek hunched his shoulders and started walking again. "It is in my family," he muttered.

Roddy could hear other people beginning to catch them up. "Listen, Marek," he started, but Marek interrupted him.

"If Mr Jenkins tries to make me change my position for good," he said fiercely. "I'll leave like Marcel did. I will," he repeated, as if trying to convince himself. "I'll leave and take up ... basketball!"

⚽ ⚽ ⚽

For the next two training sessions, Marek wasn't allowed to practise shooting. Instead, Mr Jenkins sent him off to train with the goalies for the whole time. No one said anything to Marek about it. In fact, Marek wasn't encouraging conversation about anything. Mr Jenkins seemed to be adding insult to injury by not letting him continue practising his shots. After all, there were still the subs to be announced. If Marek could raise his game, he might still get a place on the bench. But his face was shuttered, and no one knew how to open the subject.

Only Jack, as usual, tried to make things difficult, but Roddy was determined to put a stop to that. When he saw the bully coming out of the main building alone the following afternoon, he seized the opportunity and lost no time in letting Jack know how angry he was. "You just lay off Marek," he said. "You only do it because you hate seeing us all looking out for each other, Billy No-mates."

"I've got more mates than you," whined Jack, but he didn't sound very convinced.

"Brett and Andy would far rather share with anyone other than you, and you know it," Roddy said. "And it's obvious Marcel left partly because you made life so difficult for him. So why don't you do yourself a favour?"

"And what?" Jack's words were aggressive, but Roddy saw that the bully looked a bit shaken.

"Just try to get on with people," Roddy told him awkwardly. "Be nice for a change."

For a moment, Jack looked as if he might be taking in Roddy's advice. Then he sniffed, and curled his lip. "Being nice never got me anywhere," he snarled.

Roddy gave up and let him go, then continued on his way with a sigh. He knew that Jack must be feeling terrible about not making the starting line-up. Maybe once the subs were announced he'd become a bit more bearable. But what if he didn't make it? Could he get any worse?

9. Marek's Dilemma

The match against Banks on Saturday was a strange one. Neither side had their minds fully on the game in hand. Despite Sam's touchline guidance, Charlton failed to score for the first time ever, and slid to a 0–0 draw. Even Keira had to admit that she was concentrating more on the Leeds game. Their first big match was now tantalisingly close.

It was a very nervy practice that Monday, as everyone knew that the subs were going to be announced. After the usual run, Mr Jenkins had them in balanced groups playing five-a-side games. He spent the rest of the time going round each group, watching them closely. It was all right for the students who'd already been selected. Their places were safe, unless they were unlucky enough to pick up an injury, but Roddy could imagine what it was like for everyone else. It must be nerve-wracking knowing this was their last chance to impress.

At the end, everyone gathered round Mr Jenkins without waiting to be called. The team members were just as excited as everyone else to find out who was going to be on the bench, ready to play at a moment's notice.

"OK then," said Mr Jenkins, flipping over the pages of the notebook he always carried with him. "Jack Carr, Polly Ratcliffe, Ashanti Nagel, John Finnigan. I want you all on the bench. Marek, can I have a word please?"

Marek and Mr Jenkins went off to one side, and the coach put his hand on Marek's shoulder.

On the Spot

Roddy looked at Geno. "Why's he talking to Marek alone?" he asked. "It's not like he's the only one who's missed out."

"Haven't a clue," said Geno.

Whatever Mr Jenkins wanted to say to Marek was soon done, because the next minute he was back with the group again.

"OK, tomorrow in training we'll have the first team taking on all comers," he said. "The rest of the year will be split into three sides, and you'll take turns against them. That'll let me get a good look at the team as a whole." Then he pushed his notebook into his jacket pocket and disappeared in the direction of the main building.

Several people gave Marek questioning glances, but no one said anything. It wasn't until much later, when the four boys were back in their room, that he volunteered any information at all.

Marek's Dilemma

"I don't know what to do," he said.

"About what?" asked Roddy.

"Mr Jenkins."

Roddy waited impatiently.

"He's said I can be on the bench for the match against Leeds, but only if I'm a sub for the goalkeeper. With Tom still out and the Stiles goalie off form, there's only really Dij to put in goal. Mr Jenkins said he'd do his best to give me the second half as keeper, if we're winning."

"So *that's* why he took you off to one side," said Roddy. "We thought he was just commiserating with you."

"No," said Marek. "He wants me to be in the squad, but as a substitute goalie."

"So there's no chance of being subbed on as a striker?" said Jimmy.

"He's got enough people up front," said Roddy. "There's Geno and Eric Bullard, and

Long Shot

John as a sub, and Keira and me, I suppose. He's right. Our real weakness is in defence. We need you as a goalie, Marek."

"But if I say yes, I'm turning my back on scoring goals for ever," said Marek despondently. "I just know it."

"Well," said Roddy, determined to be positive. "How does that make you feel ... if you take your family out of the equation," he added hastily.

"Yes," Geno said. "Forget them for the moment. Which position do you enjoy playing in most?"

Marek folded his arms. "Well, you can't beat scoring," he told them. "You know what it's like, Geno, and you, too, Roddy. It's such a thrill to get the ball in the net. Everyone cheers, and you feel so great... It's fantastic." He lifted up the Polish flag from where it lay on his bed, and stared at it. "I wanted to score goals for my country," he said. "But maybe Żurawski was wrong. Maybe you *can't* always do what you want, however hard you try." He dropped the flag, and smoothed it out over the bed again. "I do enjoy keeping," he admitted. "I know I've tried not to, but ... more importantly, I want us to have the best possible chance of beating Leeds. I never thought I'd say it, but maybe my future doesn't lie in being a striker after all.

"I don't know what I'm going to say to my cousin when he turns up for the match," he said heavily. "I know he'll be doubly shocked. First that I'm on the bench, and about my change of position, too. But ... I think I have to go for it, don't I?"

"Yes!" Roddy leaped up and punched the air.

"Good decision!" said Geno, grinning wildly.

Long Shot

"It'll be great to have you in defence," said Jimmy, looking relieved. "We work well together."

"Thank you," said Marek. "And for putting up with me. I know I've been a real pain recently."

"It's hardly surprising," said Roddy. "It must be really odd to start out in one position and then discover you're better at a totally different one. But Mr Jenkins is right. We need you as a goalie, Marek."

⚽ ⚽ ⚽

The next morning in training, the first team lined up all together, and Mr Jenkins gave them some final advice about playing as a team. "I know it's a little strange playing alongside people who are your rivals in house matches, but that's exactly what it's like playing international football.

"You're on the same team now, and

you've got to leave your house differences behind. So let's see how you do, and I'll give you advice as you need it."

Mr Jenkins was right, it *was* strange lining up alongside Moore, Stiles and Banks players. They'd all played together in small practice games before, but not a proper 11-a-side match. But at least Roddy knew he could rely on Keira beside him in the middle of the pitch.

Stadium School are getting ready for their first match of the season, and the ball is played back to captain Sanders from the kickoff. She brings it forward through the centre circle, then passes it square to Jones. The pass is intercepted by an opposing player, however, and suddenly the Stadium School defence is threatened. Piper comes charging out, but the ball is already gone, passed out to the wing. A swirling cross comes back in,

On the Spot

and with Piper stranded outside the box it's a free header. Luckily for Stadium School, Anichebe makes a comfortable save, but that wasn't the start they had in mind.

Mr Jenkins signalled for a time out. "Jimmy, the defence has to play as a unit," he explained. "You always need to know where the rest of the back four is, and be sure they're covering all the attackers before you go wandering out like that. Dij will coordinate you as much as he can, but try to keep it tight. You can't play them offside on your own. And Roddy, as good as you are going forward, in a 4–4–2 there's nobody covering the defence if you and Keira both rush up the other end. You need to be disciplined, and stay back sometimes." Mr Jenkins blew his whistle to restart the game, and immediately the team started playing better.

Marek's Dilemma

Patel with the ball now on the left wing for Stadium School, and he's managed to shake off his marker. He gets past another defender – what a great run! He slides the ball into the path of Bullard, who is forced wide by the centre back. He tries a shot, but the angle is too narrow and it's a routine save for Dvorski in the opposing team's goal.

"Don't be afraid to pass, Eric," called Mr Jenkins. "Geno was in a better position to score. Sometimes you can't take the glory yourself. Play for the team!"

As the training session went on, the team grew in confidence. And by the time they had scored their third goal in the last practice game, Roddy felt more than ready to meet Leeds for the big match on Wednesday.

10. The Big Match

The weather wasn't kind on match day. It had rained heavily in the night, and now an icy wind was slicing through the trees.

Every match against other schools and academies was played on the original Stadium pitch. So, in spite of the sodden conditions, Roddy wasn't worried about the quality of the playing surface. In fact, he couldn't wait to get his first run out on to the pitch. He knew that the ground would be perfect – the pitch was the pride of the school.

Both teams were lined up at the changing-room end of the tree-lined avenue, which marked the site of the original players' tunnel. The trees were sheltering them from the worst of the wind, but Roddy knew that as soon as they went on to the pitch it would hit them hard.

He shot a glance at Keira. Their captain looked uncharacteristically pale, but she was also fired up for her team's first outing. She caught his glance and grinned back excitedly.

Geno was smiling, too. Nothing seemed to be bothering him. Ali and Eric were too busy jumping up and down to keep warm to respond. Dij looked rather awed by the occasion. They would certainly miss Tom Larsson's safe pair of hands.

Roddy looked curiously at the Leeds players. If anything, they seemed more nervous. But then it was an away match for them. At least Roddy and his team-mates were in familiar surroundings.

The word was given, and the teams

started to move down the avenue. As they reached the pitch, every Stadium School player reached out and touched the back of the nearest pitch-side seat. It was supposed to be lucky to touch these original stadium seats, the only ones left after the fire.

And then they were running out on to the turf. Roddy glanced at the dugout, where the subs were waiting in their tracksuits. Marek was talking to a man, who was leaning over the back of the dugout. That must be his cousin.

Keira ran to the centre, where the ref was waiting. He tossed a coin and the opposing captain called. Leeds chose to start. Keira dropped back and waited for the whistle. They were off.

We're here today at Stadium School for this mid-week match. Leeds kick off and are passing the ball around well, not letting their

The Big Match

opponents get a look in. Leeds are searching for an opening in the Stadium School defence, and when they find one, they are capable of attacking with pace and numbers. Toby Harris, the Stadium School full-back slips on the wet turf, and immediately the Leeds winger is around him and preparing to cross. Four Leeds players have popped up in the penalty area, and the ball is hoisted in towards them. Piper heads it away, but another Leeds player, loitering just outside the box, fizzes a shot back in. It flies just over the crossbar, but had it been a foot lower, Anichebe would have had no chance. That's an early warning for Stadium School.

Anichebe takes the goal kick, and the game settles into a midfield battle, with Leeds dominating slightly. Jones and Sanders are working tirelessly for Stadium School, but this Leeds team may be just too much for *them today. Jones loses the ball, and the white-shirted Leeds players are streaming forward again. They burst through the defence, and Anichebe has no chance as he's left two against one. He moves out towards the player with the ball, but a simple pass and finish leaves the ball in the back of the net. 1–0 to Leeds.*

Dij bawled at the defence, but it was nobody's fault. The pace of the Leeds attack had been formidable.

The teams form up in their own halves, and it's Perotti with the kickoff, to Bullard. Bullard looks around and sees Patel surging forward down the left wing. He knocks a lovely ball for him to run on to, and Patel reaches it well before the defenders. He takes a second to see where the rest of his team is, then runs into trouble and is forced to play it back to Jones. Leeds are putting pressure on Stadium School every time they get the ball, and making it difficult for them to put any moves together. Jones is shielding the ball well with his body, though, and keeping possession for his team. Sanders is there to support him now, and he plays the ball to her. Sanders gets free with a burst of pace, but her pass is blown off course by the wind and goes out of play.

Stadium School were really struggling, especially with the bad weather. Playing long passes was all but impossible, but running with the ball was also difficult, thanks to the slippery grass. Leeds were happy to be a goal up, and concentrated on disrupting any attempts Stadium School made to get forward.

Another Stadium School attack breaks down, and Leeds are on the hunt for a second goal. Their captain splits the Stadium

Long Shot

School defence with a brilliant pass, and the Leeds striker claims his second goal with ease. 2–0 to Leeds. And Stadium School are in trouble.

Dij kicked the ball glumly down the field, and Roddy knew just how he felt. They were losing, it was nearly half-time and it didn't look as if they would be able to get back into the game. The rest of the team looked just as miserable as he did, and it was a relief when the whistle blew and they could all take a break. It was going to take something very special to turn the game around.

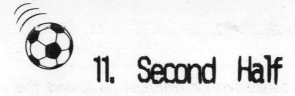

11. Second Half

Mr Jenkins was waiting for them in the team-talk room.

"Two goals down at half-time doesn't have to be the end of the story," he told them, handing out drinks and biscuits. "Ball control is tricky for both teams in these conditions, and long passes are the hardest. You're safer making short passes and finding yourselves space. Keep supporting each other and try not to give Leeds the chance to use the ball." Mr Jenkins turned to Dij. "You've got a tough job out there, but you're coping well. Two goals isn't bad, it could easily have been a lot more. It's not your fault they've been all over us."

On the Spot

Roddy was sorry that Marek wouldn't get his chance to play, but obviously Mr Jenkins thought he was too much of a risk when they were two goals down.

"Leeds are a bit weaker on your side of the pitch, Ali," Mr Jenkins continued. "You've had some good possession, but the wind has whipped the ball out of play when you've passed it. Hang on to it a bit longer, until you can get closer to Geno. If you keep giving him the chances, he's going to get at least one in. Keira, be ready to scoop up any loose balls from Ali and get them back to Geno as well."

He looked encouragingly at them all. "Leeds might come back out feeling complacent," he said, "and if you play a strong, attacking game you may well catch them on the hop. Aim for two quick goals, before they have a chance to settle down.

And then we'll get some fresh legs on for the final push. Believe you can do it and you will!"

"You heard Mr Jenkins," Keira urged her team. "We can still beat them. Come on!"

No changes at the start of the second half, with the Stadium School coach trusting the team he has to get the job done. They kick off, and immediately set about getting back into the game. Jones passes to Barker, who cuts inside and passes to Sanders. Sanders sprays it out to Patel, who beats two men before whipping in a cross. A defender gets there first and cuts it out, but is forced to put the ball behind for a corner. This is much more positive play from Stadium School, and Leeds will have to be careful. Jones takes the corner, and it finds its way to Perotti. Perotti shoots, but the keeper gets a hand to it. A defender tries to hack it away, but Bullard is there and thrashes it into the net. A scrappy goal, but it counts. 2–1, and Stadium School are back in with a shout.

The home crowd cheered wildly, and Eric ran over to the corner flag, where Roddy was standing, to high-five him.

But Keira cut them short. "We're still a goal down!" she said. "We've got a lot more to do before we can start celebrating."

Leeds restart the game, and that goal seems to have got their blood pumping again. Almost immediately they are pushing for a goal, and their striker is one on one with the keeper. Anichebe dives bravely down at the striker's feet, stopping a certain goal.

Roddy halted his run as play stopped. "What's happened?" he asked Keira.

"Dij. I think he got a kick to his head," she gasped, catching her breath. "It looks as if Marek will have to be subbed on after all."

Second Half

Roddy watched as Dij got groggily to his feet with the help of Mrs Anstruther. Keira was right. Mr Jenkins was speaking to Marek, and now Marek was changing out of his tracksuit and getting warmed up on the touchline.

And so the substitute keeper takes his place in goal for the team. There is no time for him to warm up properly, and Leeds will be looking to exploit that. Dvorski puts on his gloves and prepares for action. Leeds sportingly give the ball back to Stadium School from the throw in, and it's passed back to Dvorski so he can get an early feel for it. He keeps the ball at his feet for a few seconds, before lumping it up the field to his team. Leeds intercept it, though, and work their way back towards the goal. A shot flies in from long range, but Dvorski is equal to it and makes a comfortable save. He rolls it out to Harris, and Stadium School enter a period of possession.

"Nice one, Marek," shouted Roddy. "Keep it up!"

Marek had made a solid save, and would be feeling more confident now. Roddy saw Marek's cousin applauding, too, which would give him a great boost.

As the minutes ticked by, Marek made save after save to keep them in the game, but at the other end of the pitch, there was less success. Geno was subbed off for John Finnigan, and Ali came off for Ashanti, as Mr Jenkins tried to find the equaliser. Fresh legs didn't quite seem to be able to do it, and the clock was running down. The ref had just signalled for two minutes of injury time when Roddy got the ball and saw the defence open up.

Jones sees a space in front of him, and

drives forward into it. He surges almost into the penalty area before he is challenged, forcing him to pass back to Sanders. Sanders lines up a long shot, but is clattered from behind just as she enters the box. There are shouts for a penalty, but the ref waves them away and points to just outside the area. It's a free kick in the dying seconds for Stadium School!

Keira stood up, but grimaced and sat down again heavily. It was no good. She would have to go off, leaving Stadium School with only ten players on the pitch. As she hobbled past Roddy, she threw him her captain's armband.

Roddy was so surprised that he didn't catch it, and the armband fell onto the grass. He picked it up in a daze, and then he realised what was happening. This was it. This was his chance to show that he was

On the Spot

worthy of being captain, even though it was in the dying moments of the match.

And now it was up to him who would take the vital free kick. He looked around at the players he could choose from. Keira had been the best, but she was standing on the touchline, no doubt willing him to make the right decision. Roddy knew that she might have picked him, but he was absolutely knackered after playing his heart out, and didn't trust himself to deliver. No one else was particularly good, except for...

"Marek!" Roddy yelled at the top of his voice, but his goalie didn't seem to have heard. Roddy was almost totally blown, but he jogged a few yards towards his own goal. Jimmy came running up to meet him.

"What do you want?" Jimmy asked Roddy.

"I need Marek," said Roddy. "I want him to take the free kick."

Second Half

"Really? Why?"

"Because," Roddy panted. "Look, just get him will you. The ref's going to do us for time wasting otherwise."

Jimmy raced off, and soon Marek was hurtling towards his captain.

"No time to talk," panted Roddy at Marek's questioning expression. "We're almost on full time. Give it all you've got. Good luck!"

"Thanks." Marek's face spoke volumes. If he messed up, everyone would blame Roddy for letting him take the free kick. But Roddy was sure he could do it. All Marek needed was someone to have confidence in him. With his cousin watching as well, surely he'd get it right.

"Don't let me down, Marek," said Roddy under his breath. "I know you can do this. Take your time."

Long Shot

In a bizarre twist, vice-captain Roddy Jones has called Dvorski, the substitute keeper forward to take this crucial free kick. All the injury time has been played, so this will be the last touch of the game, and the last chance for Stadium School to draw level. Dvorski takes a deep breath and begins his run-up, but is halted by the referee.

Roddy watched in agony as the ref objected to the position of the wall. He waved them back, and paced out a careful ten yards from the ball. Roddy was sure he'd die if the wait had put Marek off his stride. It seemed ages until the ref was satisfied, and by then the atmosphere was electric.

The Leeds goalie is shifting nervously on the goal line, and Dvorski sets himself up again. He trots up to the ball, and hammers it full-pelt towards the goal.

Roddy could hardly bear to watch, but his

eyes were glued to the ball as it left Marek's boot.

John Finnigan moves from his position in the Leeds wall. How has the ball found that gap?

Everyone's heart was in their mouth as the ball smashed in off the post, and spun all the way along the back of the net.

Two goals apiece. Stadium School have equalised with the last kick of the game! What a fantastic recovery.

The cheers were so loud it was almost impossible to hear the final whistle.

Ashanti came up to Roddy and gave him a huge, muddy hug.

"We did it! Honours even!"

But Roddy was looking for Marek. He should be taking the praise. It had been a scorcher of a goal.

"Where's Marek?" he asked Jimmy.

On the Spot

Jimmy pointed behind Roddy, and Roddy turned to see Marek still running back to cover his goal, like a good goalkeeper should do. He couldn't have waited to see if the shot had gone home, and he certainly couldn't have heard the whistle.

"Marek. Marek!" For the second time, Roddy was yelling at his keeper.

At last Marek heard and turned around. He looked at Roddy in surprise. "Is it over?" he asked.

Ashanti and John beat Roddy to it. They were slapping Marek's back and cheering, and Jimmy rushed over to do the same. By the time Roddy reached them, Marek was grinning.

"We did it!" he yelled to Roddy. "We got the equaliser!"

"*You* did it," corrected Roddy. "You scored that vital goal, and kept loads out. You see?

Second Half

You *can* do both!"

Marek grinned. He pointed to where his cousin was cheering wildly. "If that doesn't please my family, I don't know what will," he said. "Thanks. You didn't have to choose me."

Roddy shook his head. "It *had* to be you," he said. "Keira was injured, John's rather unpredictable at free kicks, and my legs were knackered. I couldn't have steadied myself enough to take it. You were the best person to take the shot. And you did it perfectly!"

Roddy shook hands with the Leeds captain and proudly led his team off the pitch. They might not have won the match, but they hadn't lost it, either. All in all, it was a great result.

At the edge of the pitch, he ran his hand over the old and very charred Stadium seat.

On the Spot

"Lucky," he muttered to himself as he did so. "When they showed us round here before I won my place at the school ... they said these seats were lucky, especially this one. Now I think it must be true!"

Available Now!

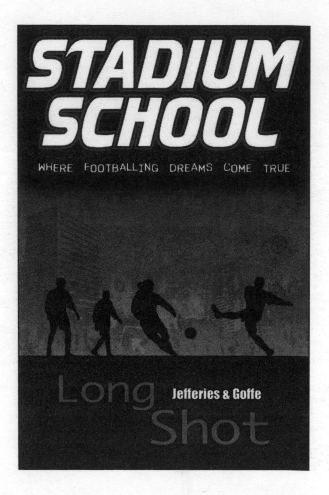

Available Now!